Zoo Day ¡Olé!

A Counting Book

by
**Phillis
Gershator**

illustrated by
**Santiago
Cohen**

Marshall Cavendish Children

Marshall Cavendish Corporation
99 White Plains Road, Tarrytown, NY 10591
www.marshallcavendish.us/kids

Library of Congress Cataloging-in-Publication Data
Gershator, Phillis.
Zoo day: !ole! : a counting book / by Phillis Gershator ; illustrated by Santiago Cohen. – 1st ed.
p. cm.
ISBN 978-0-7614-5462-5
1. Counting–Juvenile literature. I. Cohen, Santiago. II. Title.
QA113.G47 2008
513.2'11–dc22
2008010783

The illustrations are rendered in ink line drawn by hand on paper and colored in Photoshop.
Book design by Vera Soki
Editor: Margery Cuyler

Printed in China
First edition
1 3 5 6 4 2

 Marshall Cavendish
Children

Mil gracias to Santiago, Margery, David, and Mimi
—P.G.

Para la abuelita Lilli con todo mi amor
—S.C.

Abuelita is coming!
We're going to the zoo.
Abuelita counts in Spanish.
Uno, dos means one and two.

Abuelita counts in Spanish.
She counts everything we see.

Uno, dos **means** one **and** two –

and tres means three.

Abuelita counts the bears.
I'm helping her keep score.
Tres means three –

and cuatro means four.

Abuelita counts the seals
splashing when they dive.
Cuatro means four —

and **cinco** means **five**

Abuelita counts the monkeys
doing monkey tricks.
Cinco means **five** –

and seis means six.

Abuelita counts the parrots perched in Treetop Heaven.

Seis means six

and siete means seven.

Abuelita counts the animals
waiting by the gate.
Siete means seven –

and ocho means eight.

Abuelita counts the people
in the ice cream line.
Ocho means eight –

and nueve means nine.

Abuelita counts the birds:
peacocks, pigeons, wren.
Nueve means nine —

and diez means ten.

Abuelita counts ten animals
all around the zoo.

Abuelita counts in Spanish, and I count in Spanish, too.

uno

dos

tres

cuatro

cinco

seis

siete

ocho

nueve

diez

The animals are sleepy now.
We say adiós, good-bye,

and count the little stars
shining in the sky.

We count the little stars
so far away and bright.

Abuelita counts in Spanish . . .

. . . and kisses me good night.

Dos besos means two kisses,

and two kisses mean sleep tight.